A CAT
AT
DACHAU

ELYSE HOFFMAN

ISBN (ebook): 978-1-952742-24-8

Project 613 Publishing
elysehoffman.com

PROJECT613

To my father Richard,
My mother Lydia
My sister Liana
My dear friend Steffi for going with me to Dachau
Our lovely tour guide Eric whose excellent work inspired this
story.
And God, Who makes all stories.

A CAT AT DACHAU

The guards at Dachau concentration camp had been trained to regard the prisoners as less than animals. Any soul that ventured through the gate which boasted *Arbeit Macht Frei, Work Makes You Free,* would be worked like a dog, beaten like a donkey, and killed like a rat.

Real animals, however, rarely ventured through the gate unless they were one of the guards' German shepherds, the ones trained to maul Jews to death. And so when SS Private Max Schrader saw a few of his fellow guards clustered near the front gate one frigid December morning in Dachau, he was surprised to see what they were gawking at.

"A cat?" he mumbled, and indeed, a tiny orange tabby that looked worse than most of the prisoners was huddled against the wide-open front gate. Its fur was matted and caked with mud and blood, multiple wounds marred its skinny body, and it had a nasty eye infection that made some sort of foul discharge spill from its golden eyes.

The SS troopers, many of whom were mere teenagers, were hovering around the poor creature, their typically harsh features soft with concern.

"Is it still alive?" one of them muttered.

"Of course it's still alive, look at it shaking," noted another.

"What happened?" Max blurted, elbowing his way past a few comrades, getting as close to the cat as possible.

"Don't know. He was just here when we came out," another guard muttered. It was Max's longtime friend and former classmate, Jochen, a fellow nineteen-year-old. Jochen whipped off his skull-emblazoned cap and wiped the sweat that had gathered on his forehead. "Poor little fellow. You think he's a stray?"

"Collar," one of the SS men said, gesturing to a small scarlet collar looped around the injured feline's neck.

"What's it say?" queried the youngest of the group, eighteen-year-old Heinz.

"Pick him up and check," suggested one SS officer. Heinz let out a rather girlish squeak and leapt away from the feline, tucking his arms against his chest.

"I'm not touchin' him, he might be rabid!" he cried, which caused a laugh to ripple across the group of SS men.

"Toughen up, Heinz!" Jochen commanded. "If you're afraid of a little cat, how are you going to handle being around Jews all day?"

"Not afraid of *Jews,* but I don't wanna get sick..." Heinz grumbled.

"God's sake, move over all of you! Poor thing's going to *want* to die if it has to keep listening to you blabber," Max cried, shoving Heinz out of the way and dropping to his knee in front of the poor animal. Affection immediately swelled in the SS trooper's heart when the cat looked up at him with its big golden eyes and let out a sad little chirp. Affection, and something else entirely. Some odd concoction of sadness and hope.

Max quickly gathered the little cat into his arms, and the weight of a small feline was familiar in a way that ached. Only two weeks ago, he had lost his own cat, also an orange tabby. Tiger had been that cat's name, and even though his comrades had laughed at him for mourning a cat as much as he had, it couldn't be helped. No amount of SS training could have forced Max to regard Tiger as a worthless animal and nothing more.

Tiger had been Max's best friend since he was a baby. The nineteen-year-old couldn't recall a time in his life when he hadn't sat near the fireplace with Tiger resting beside him. When Max had come home crying because of bullies or brutal teachers, the cat had scurried to the sobbing child and rubbed his fuzzy little head against his human, an assurance that he would love the lad no matter what. As an adult, training for a future in the new Reich, Max would stay up well into the night with one hand clutching *Mein Kampf* and the other petting Tiger as the aging cat snoozed in his lap.

Tiger had become fatally ill a few weeks ago, and even though Max had done everything in his power to get leave so that he could say goodbye to his pet, the Kommandant had been utterly unsympathetic. "It's just a damn cat," he had said. "We have more important things to worry about."

More important things, of course, being the war against Jews, the duty of every SS man to rip the prisoners confined in Dachau apart as thoroughly as Tiger had once torn apart mice. Max was a devoted Nazi, but he had genuinely considered quitting right then so that he could be with Tiger in his final hours.

He hadn't, though, and Tiger had died without him, and that knowledge had made Max unable to sleep for two weeks.

But here, it seemed, was a chance at redemption practically plopped into his lap: a little cat that would have looked just like Tiger if he weren't so terribly skinny and injured.

"All right, little fellow," Max crooned, letting the trembling cat nestle against his SS jacket. "It's all right. Good boy, good kitten. Did you get lost? Where's your human?"

A few of his comrades chuckled. Jochen was smirking in amusement. "Soft," he mouthed, and Max rolled his eyes. He had been called soft by his fellow SS men plenty of times in the past: because of his love for his cat, because he had cried when Tiger died, because he hated it when the Kommandant hit the guard dogs.

It was nonsense, really. The Führer, who loved animals—the propaganda outlets never tired of showing pictures of Hitler feeding dogs and deer and birds—would have surely supported his soldier showing German goodness towards an innocent animal.

"Maybe he belongs to one of the villagers," suggested

Jochen, gesturing in the vague direction of the town of Dachau. "Collar?"

Max glanced at the tag on the collar, which wasn't helpful at all: it didn't offer an address or a phone number, only a name in gothic font: "*Faust.*"

"Faust. Huh. Good name for this place, I guess," quipped Max, which earned a few chuckles from his fellow SS men.

"Maybe he can be our new mascot if his owner abandoned him," suggested Heinz, and Max shrugged, marching through the *Arbeit Macht Frei* gate.

"Maybe! The vet might know his owner!" Max cried as he took off towards the village of Dachau. "Jochen, cover for me!"

"Hey, wha—?" Jochen started to object, but Max didn't hear any of his friend's bellyaching as the cat let out a small "meow" of protest that made the SS man's typically iron heart swell with affection.

"Don't you worry, little fellow," he said. "We'll find your human, and if not, I'll be your human. You'll like it here at Dachau. Plenty of mice and plenty of nice people."

THE VET IN DACHAU VILLAGE DID NOT RECOGNIZE LITTLE Faust, though she declared that he must have had an owner at some point: he wasn't a kitten, but an adult cat that obviously didn't know how to get by without a human's love and care.

"Abandoned?" suggested Max, stroking the poor cat's head and muttering words of comfort while the vet readied a fluid injection.

"Abandoned, maybe, or his owner may have been unable to care for him any longer and just let him out," she said. Faust squirmed and let out a yowl of discomfort while the vet slid the needle into his little arm. Max wrinkled his nose and shook his head.

"I would hope not, and if he did, why wouldn't he take the collar off?"

"The alternative is that his owner was elderly and may have passed away, and the cat may have just wandered after that. Maybe he just got lost and his owner's fine. Unfortunately, without an address, there's really no way to track down his old family. Not until he gets better, anyway. Once he's better, he may very well go off and try to find his old owner again."

"That's his choice," said Max with a shrug and a small smile. Most of his comrades in the SS valued dogs for their loyalty, and when they had learned that Max was more of a cat person, they had laughed at him for loving such seemingly disloyal animals. "Dogs will die for you," Jochen, who had two dogs, had declared with pride. "Cats, you're lucky if they stay around long enough to watch you die."

Max, though, had always preferred the character of a cat. Cats loved just as thoroughly as dogs, but their love was selective and subtle. Love that was difficult to earn was more valuable to Max. Every time Tiger had greeted him with utter affection, he had been filled with a sense of accomplishment.

Of course, SS training was effectively about making the cadets into loyal dogs that would bite and maul without hesitation or question. The aloof cat, ever watchful, ever independent, was anathema to the spirit of the Nazi movement. An SS man who acted like a cat, who carefully observed and escaped if things weren't good, was a failure of an SS man.

"If you're intending on adopting the cat, Herr, I'll need to know now so we can fill out the proper paperwork," the vet said.

"And so I can foot the bill?" chuckled Max, and the vet let out a non-committal hum that became a small sigh of relief as Max yanked out his ID card.

"I'm guarding the camp," he said. "Discount?"

"Discount for our brave soldiers," the vet confirmed with a smile. "Do you want to change the name?"

"Faust is fine for him," Max said, tucking his ID away and waving towards the vet's expensive medications. "Do whatever you have to."

"Didn't know they paid you so well at the camp."

"They *don't.*"

"Good thing you're getting a discount, then."

"He'll be okay?" Max said, his voice softening as he petted little Faust's head, eliciting a purr from the feline which made him feel a great sense of triumph. The vet nodded.

"With your generous intervention, your cat will be just fine, Herr Schrader."

IT WAS DIFFICULT TO DISCERN THE CHARACTER OF AN animal while it was under sedation, but as the weeks marched on and little Faust's health grew stronger and stronger, Max found that his new pet had the personality of hard candy: tough but sweet.

Faust was certainly a stubborn soul—very much like Tiger in that regard, who had never suffered to be pet or coddled for longer than he wished before the claws came out. Unlike Tiger, however, Faust was all hiss and no swipe. He would bare his fangs and let out a snake-like sound whenever the vet drew near with another tool to prod, poke and heal, but even when she manhandled him, he never scratched.

At the same time, Faust seemed to realize that Max was his savior, and almost as soon as he could stand on his own, the cat would totter over to the SS man and press his forehead against Max's. He greeted the SS man with a loud purr every time he saw him, and when Max managed to get the vet's permission to hold his new pet, Faust curled up against the Nazi and refused to be moved for two straight hours.

The precious little cat was certainly worth the trouble —and he was a lot of trouble, though not through any fault of his own. The medicine for his eye infection alone devoured Max's savings, even with the Dachau-guard discount. Max stopped going out with his friends for drinks, which saved some money but not nearly enough. He was forced to call his parents and ask for his birthday and Christmas gifts early in the form of funds for Faust's vet bills.

When that wasn't enough, however, Max waited until

he found a Jew with one shimmering gold tooth still stuck in his mouth and punched him, knocking the tooth out. That paid for the rest of Faust's vet bills, as well as his food, some toys, and a nice little scratching post. It also got Max a day off since he claimed that the Jew had cursed Hitler.

The Jew was punished for that made-up offense, of course. He got *Twenty-Five*, and after that, he died. Max couldn't care less about that, though. A subhuman was worth far less than the comfort of a cute little cat.

IT TOOK TIME, LOVE, MONEY, AND A JEW'S LIFE, BUT eventually, Faust was cleared to go home with his new owner. And since his new owner was a young SS cadet, his new home was going to be the Dachau concentration camp. Or, rather, the SS barracks just outside the camp, where Max and his comrades were quartered.

It was a pleasant white building decorated with SS banners that was a slight distance from the *Arbeit Macht Frei* gate where Max had first found Faust. Nice, quiet, far from the electrified barbed wire that kept the prisoners hostage. Faust would be perfectly safe.

Technically, of course, the guards' barracks were not a place for pets: the most that the SS cadets were typically allowed by way of personalization was a poster or a plant to try and make their little space a bit more homey, and even that was usually frowned upon. The guards were not there to show individuality: "Dachau isn't a damn boarding school," the Kommandant would usually say if one of the guards tried to put up a drawing made by their child or a gift sent by their girlfriend.

Despite this, it was actually relatively easy for Max to convince the Kommandant to let him keep Faust in the barracks: rats and mice were always an issue, even far from the camp grounds, and any means of fighting them was welcome so long as it didn't disrupt anything.

Faust took to scratching at his little scratching post right away, so there was no fear that he would ruin the guards' chairs or mattresses. He was litter trained, well-behaved, and therefore welcome in the barracks.

Quickly, the rest of the Dachau guards took a liking to the little cat. It soon became clear that Faust was going to be fat from every guard giving him scraps of chicken during lunch and dinner. Even Jochen conceded that Faust was all right for a cat and ended up bringing him little toys fashioned from yarn and sticks.

Faust was utterly spoiled, and though he showed his affection to all of the SS men who fed and played with him, Max was clearly his human, his favorite. When Max strode into the room, Faust would rush to him, rub against his dusty jackboots, and offer a rumbling purr.

Soon, Max discovered his cat's quirks. Tiger had loved cheese above everything else, but Faust, oddly, went crazy for croissants. The SS guards soon learned that they couldn't eat a croissant in their barrack without sharing lest they be hassled by the little feline. Tiger had typically slept on Max's bed, but even though Faust had a plethora of beds to choose from, he decided that he preferred sleeping in one of the bathroom sinks. This was also where he got his water, and Jochen confessed that watching the cat drink from the faucet was "pretty damn cute."

Max quickly discovered something else about his cat: Faust was an escape artist of the highest caliber. He didn't intend to let the cat roam the outdoors, but somehow, the cat managed to escape his new home almost every single day, and once he was out, he would immediately bolt for the camp and slip through the *Arbeit Macht Frei* gate.

This was initially concerning, because Dachau concentration camp was certainly no place for a cat. The poor little cat needed peace and quiet, and there was no quiet in Dachau. There was always barking, cursing, and the loudspeakers spread all across the camp would constantly blare Nazi music and Hitler speeches in an attempt to either brainwash the prisoners or, more likely, torture them even more by forbidding them from getting even a second of reprieve from Nazism.

It was also potentially quite dangerous in Dachau. There were sharp things lying everywhere, barracks with hand-sized splinters. There was the crematorium that was always running, always on fire. There were the guard dogs that were trained to kill, and Max was terrified that one of them would get loose and maul poor Faust.

Then, of course, there were Jews. The greatest danger of them all in Max's mind. The propaganda he consumed willingly at home and unwillingly when he listened to the loudspeakers during his workday always told him that wicked Jews were horribly cruel to the most innocent—German women, German children, and yes, even German animals. Jews, evil as they were, took delight in torturing animals for their odd rituals. Jews, who couldn't love but could only destroy and therefore needed to be destroyed, those Jews would surely kick or hit the poor cat if they got the opportunity.

Nevertheless, Max knew from life experience that there was no wrangling a cat, and so the only thing he could do was try to keep an eye on Faust. This proved easy enough: Faust stuck out quite a bit in the otherwise gloomy camp. The cat would wander about the grounds, going from barrack to barrack, building to building. He spent a concerning amount of time near the crematorium.

Nobody bothered him, though, because it was clear that the cat was searching for something: as he skittered about the camp, Faust would always be sniffing the ground and the walls. The SS guards assumed that the cat was merely hunting down the rats and mice infesting the camp, which made him popular with both the prisoners and the Nazis.

Max, however, realized quite quickly that this wasn't the case, though of course he didn't say as much to his superiors who tolerated the cat's presence. Cats, he knew, were silent hunters, and Faust was not silent at all when he stalked through Dachau. Throughout the day, the cat would march across the camp and let out an unearthly, long, particular call: "Mrerow! Mrerow!"

Such a call would have surely scared off any mice, and any cat that was a decent hunter would have known better. Which meant that either Faust was a particularly terrible hunter or, more likely, he was hunting for something besides mice. Something important enough that when Max's workday ended and the cat followed him home, the cat's tail would be low, his gait slowed, his every movement communicating his disappointment.

MORNINGS IN DACHAU WENT LIKE THIS: ROLL-CALL. IN the *Appellplatz*, the vast stretch of land between the maintenance building and the barracks, the prisoners, all rendered identical by their shared dehumanization— shaved heads, wooden clogs, striped outfits—would gather and stand in rows of ten.

Any prisoner that had died during the night had to be dragged out and put in his spot, rendering the rows less even and making roll-call last much longer than it should have, which mattered a great deal to the prisoners being accounted for. roll-call was a torture all its own.

Rain, sleet, or blistering cold, it didn't matter: they all had to stand out there in their paper-thin prisoners' garments. Even if the roll-call took hours, the Jews were not permitted to break from a particular, humiliating pose: hands at sides, legs together, head bowed. No hands in pockets, that would get them *Twenty-Five*. No looking up, that would also get them *Twenty-Five*.

Max was an observant man, and he would notice these little infractions. Some of his comrades would personally flog any prisoner that tucked their freezing hands into their pockets, but Max didn't. It was a bother, and it always made him lose count, which meant that the entire roll-call would have to start over again, which meant that more prisoners would drop from exhaustion, which meant more beatings, more time, and on and on.

And Max hated roll-call, not because it killed Jews, but because it was *boring*. He wanted to get it over with.

Twenty-Five was easier. Two words, and then he didn't have to think about it.

Max rarely got distracted, but one day while he was counting, a familiar noise interrupted the sound of his voice yelling numbers and the din of Nazi music blaring over the intercom system. "Mrerow! Mreeereeeow!"

Max paused his count (which was cruel because that made roll-call go on just a bit longer.) His gaze glided towards the sound of his cat's voice. There was Faust, no longer searching but sitting right in front of one particular Jewish man, a prisoner who may have once been young but whose time at the camp had aged him ten years.

There didn't seem to be anything special about the Jew that Faust had selected: he looked like all the others with his shaved head, sallow cheeks, striped uniform, and dead eyes. But Faust must have somehow recognized him because he sat in front of him, meowing insistently.

For a moment, Max was both confused and concerned that the Jew would kick the poor cat, but the prisoner didn't. He looked at Faust, exhausted eyes brightening slightly even as he didn't dare say a word or break from his mandatory pose. Even when Faust started rubbing against the Jew's legs like he did with the SS men he lived with, the Jew knew better than to move.

Curiosity took hold of Max's soul, which was bad. Curiosity was for cats, and Enemies of the State who asked too many questions and didn't just *listen* and *follow orders.*

Nevertheless, he quickly jotted down the particular Jew's number. He finished roll-call, and when the Jews were splitting into their work details, Max ran to Heinz, who would be overseeing the group of the Jew that Faust had seemingly recognized.

"Hey, that Jew, send him to interrogation," Max commanded.

"Why?" Heinz queried with a raised brow, and Max certainly didn't have a good answer to that. *Because he might be Faust's owner. Because something's off and I need to figure out what.* No good answer, and so he just offered to pay for Heinz's drinks tonight if he obliged, and that did the trick.

"Ha! Fine! You, Jew!"

Initially, and perhaps wisely, the Jew did not go quietly. He cried and begged for mercy, and his pleas were met with a smack in the chest from Heinz's bull-whip. Faust started yowling when the Jew cried out in pain, however, and Max intervened because hearing the cat's distress made his heart ache.

"Jew, you're not getting *Twenty-Five*, come on!" he snapped, grabbing the trembling man by the arm and yanking him towards the building reserved for interrogations. Max heard the Jew let out a small sigh of relief. The prisoner didn't fight as the SS man dragged him away from his work group.

Max left the Jew sitting in the interrogation room and ran to his locker, grabbing his satchel. When he returned to the interrogation building, he found Faust scratching at the door and letting out that particular cry: "Mrerow! Mrerow!"

"Easy, Faust," Max sighed, scooping the cat into his arms and carrying him into the building. Max felt like a phone operator trying to connect a line to a slot that didn't exist. He certainly would have believed that poor Faust had been owned and abused by an evil, depraved Jew at some point, and it wasn't out of the question that such a monstrous owner might have ended up in Dachau, but if that was the case, why was Faust so affectionate towards this Jew? It simply didn't make any sense.

Not now. He would get to the bottom of it. Make it make sense. He opened the door to the interrogation room and found the Jew taking advantage of the single moment of relative quiet: he had his shaved head laid on the table and was shutting his eyes. The noise-proof walls of the interrogation room offered a momentary reprieve from the blaring music of the camp, and the smooth, slightly blood splattered table before him was likely far more comfortable than the rough bunk he was used to.

"Jew, up," commanded Max, and the Jew immediately lifted his head, dark eyes flitting from the SS man to the cat in his arms. Faust meowed and started squirming, but Max refused to let him go just yet.

"State your name," the SS man ordered, and the prisoner sighed, glancing down at the number sewn onto his breast to remind himself of his new identity before he began to recite, "Nine-five-seven..."

"No, no, your...*original* name," Max clarified. Faust was squirming too much, and Max was forced to gently set the cat down. The Jew's eyes briefly glinted with curiosity before he quietly muttered, "It's Saul. Saul Waldorf."

Max had never known a Jew by name before, and something about knowing this one as something other than *Jew* or a line of numbers made him feel slightly queasy. Slowly, he sat in the chair across from Saul as Faust leapt onto the table and purred loudly, rubbing his face against the prisoner's hollow cheeks. The Jew suppressed a smile and petted the cat.

"Good boy, Faust," he said, confirming that Faust's affection wasn't coming from nowhere. "Good to see *you're* all right, at least. Where did you come from?"

"He was lying near the front gate," Max said, and Saul chewed on his tongue for a moment, likely pondering exactly how stupid it would be to say what he was thinking.

Saul must have correctly guessed that Max was not in a murderous mood, because he said, "I'm surprised you didn't shoot him."

That earned a derisive scoff from the SS man, who sat up straight and spoke with all the confidence of a schoolboy reading a textbook aloud: "We Germans are one of the few races on earth who treat animals decently. Unlike Jews who mercilessly torture animals with their kosher slaughter..."

"I don't eat kosher food, so..." The prisoner rolled his boney shoulders in a non-committal fashion. "Well, I *would* eat it, if it were offered, but not *only* kosher food."

Max grunted at being interrupted by a subhuman, but curiosity won out over pride. Talk of food reminded him of his satchel. He reached into it and pulled out an offering: a croissant. Faust immediately skittered towards his Nazi owner, forgetting Saul entirely as his eyes gleamed with hungry fervor.

"Share with him," Max commanded, tossing the croissant at the prisoner and nodding his head towards Faust. He expected the Jew to bellyache about being forced to split his meager rations with a mere animal, but Saul gave an amused smile and nodded, plucking off a piece of the croissant and dropping it in front of the cat before taking a hearty bite himself.

"Silly cat," Saul said, nodding towards the cat and speaking through a mouthful of pastry. "Faust here, he's been obsessed with croissants since he was a kitten. Never went crazy for chicken or fish, but put a croissant in front of him and he...oh! Faust, come on, let me have some!"

Faust meowed in protest, shoving his face in Saul's, trying to snag a bite of the croissant as the Jew ate. The prisoner didn't seem angry at this, though: he let out a slight laugh, and Max, unable to maintain the icy mask of an SS man while observing such a ridiculous scene, let the edge of his lip twitch upwards.

"Any reason for that?" Max asked. "How long did you have him for?"

"Oh! He isn't my cat," Saul said, shaking his head and hand -feeding a small piece of croissant to Faust. "Should have clarified that. No, he's my roommate's cat."

"Roommate?" Max repeated. Saul finished off his croissant and coughed a few times. Max, by instinct, grabbed his canteen and offered it to the Jew. That was a bit odd: the SS man was used to hearing Jews choking and coughing on smoke and dirt, and never had that polite urge gripped him, the same instinct that he felt whenever a family member or a friend caught and he reached for his water.

"Jakob. Old friend from school," Saul said, setting the canteen aside once he had quenched his thirst. He smiled slightly as he spoke of his friend, one bony hand reaching out and casually petting Faust as the cat licked crumbs of croissant off the blood-stained table.

"His mother was a real harpy, kicked him out when he was fifteen," Saul explained. "He was having trouble finding work. You know, Jew and all."

Jew and all. Max remembered how difficult his father had said it was to find work as an unskilled teenager. Max had at least had the SS to fall back on, but in the Reich, of course, nobody wanted to employ a Jewish teenager. If he starved to death on the streets, all the better, after all.

"I let him sleep on my couch," Saul said. "I still had a job as a janitor at the synagogue, so that's how I got by."

"Where'd he get Faust?" Max queried, and the cat, finally finished lapping up crumbs, scooted closer to Saul and started unleashing that particular call: "Mrerow, mrerow..."

"Yeah, I know, buddy," crooned Saul before looking up at the SS man and explaining. "That's his way of asking for Jakob. He's been doing that since he was a kitten. Jakob found him under a dumpster outside our apartment complex. Found a mother cat dead a few feet away, the other kittens were dead too. I figure mama cat brought a poisoned rat home to the babies. Faust was lucky to be the runt of the litter. He didn't get any, so he survived."

"Lucky cat..." muttered Max as the cat kept calling for Jakob Beckhardt. Saul nodded.

"Very. Jakob really loved cats as a kid, apparently, but his mother never let him have one. She had this yappy little dog that drove him insane, he'd always complain about it. He was real happy to find the cat, and I couldn't say no to him. Don't even know if my landlord allowed pets, but it made him happy."

"He...was good to Faust?" muttered Max in disbelief, which fetched a gravelly laugh from the prisoner.

"Good doesn't describe it!" Saul cried. "He *loved* that cat. Oh, goodness, any extra penny he had went into the cat fund. Cat needs vet check-ups, and there was only one vet who would service Jews, and *he* charged an arm and a leg. Cat needs food, but the pet shop won't sell to Jews, so now Faust eats whatever we eat. I suspect that's how he got so obsessed with croissants: Jakob worked at a bakery most of the time and brought those home, so if we didn't have anything else to eat..."

"Croissants." Max smirked even though his training told him not to. Sharing a smile with a Jew was a sin.

"Croissants," Saul confirmed with a nod. "Oh! And! Suddenly I can't use my sink because the cat decides..."

"That's his bed." The smile was claiming more of Max's face, and when Saul's eyes really brightened, that only made it worse. There was no wall of hierarchy in shared amusement over a cat's antics, no subhuman and master race.

"He's in your sink now?" said Saul, and Max nodded. The prisoner laughed, truly laughed, which was an odd sound coming from a starving creature like him.

Scratchy and sudden, as though his throat was rejecting showing mirth in a place like this.

"That's hilarious!" Saul cried, and then the laughing stopped, the smile became bitter, and his gaze shifted from the cat to the bloodstains on the table. "At least some things don't change..."

Then, they were subhuman and master race again, and Max was filled with a sense of both relief, because it was much easier to be the master race, and something resembling disappointment, because he felt like something had been stolen from him.

"What....ah..." the SS man muttered, clearing his throat and speaking in an interrogator's tone once more. "Is Jakob Beckhardt still at your apartment? Do you know where he'd be?"

"I know where'd he'd be all right," Saul said with a shake of his head, and there was a faintly accusatory note to his voice. "Not that apartment, no. Me and him got arrested and deported together, you see. One minute we're walking into the apartment, next minute we're being dragged out and tossed into the back of a truck while some crazy mob runs in and smashes up all our furniture. I heard Faust yowl, thought he might'a gotten crushed, but Jakob said he saw him run off."

Saul paused his tale, letting his eyes flit from the cat, who was skittering about the room and sniffing the bloodstains on the wall, to the SS man before him. "He was so worried about that damn cat. Worried about what would happen to him. Doesn't surprise me...that the cat would track him all the way here. Jakob loved him, and he loved Jakob so damn much. Poor Faust."

"Poor Faust?" repeated Max, glancing at the cat,

noting the anxious swishing of the feline's tail. "Wait...if Jakob's here, where is he? Which barrack?"

"You really don't remember?" Saul said, nearly a hiss, exhausted eyes narrowing with disbelief. "It wasn't that long ago."

"*What* wasn't that long ago?" Max said, half a demand and half a frustrated plea. Saul answered, his tone carrying with it the coldness of an angel damning a sinner to Hell.

"You gave him *Twenty-Five*."

TWENTY-FIVE WAS THIS: AN INFRACTION WOULD HAPPEN, real or imagined, and an SS man would point to the offender and declare, simply, *Twenty-Five*. It was always a grand thing, calling *Twenty-Five*. It made him feel like a king condemning a helpless subject with only a word and a gesture.

Twenty-Five was lashes. It sounded simple, a punishment unworthy of the gravitas, until it was actually carried out. The victim would be tied to a wooden table like an animal, backside exposed, and then he would be beaten with a bullwhip. And while he was beaten, he would have to count—in German, in perfect German, God help him if he didn't know German—every smack of the whip severing skin from flesh and flesh from bone. *One, two, three,* all the way up to *twenty-five.*

The beating was very rarely only *twenty-five* lashes because the prisoner would scream, or stutter, or wouldn't know that twenty-one is not *zwanzig-und-ein* but *ein-und-zwanzig* because German was only their second language, and they couldn't think anything except *it hurts make it stop.*

It wouldn't stop until the prisoner counted perfectly to twenty-five. If they couldn't, it went on until they passed out, and when they woke up, it would start again.

Twenty-Five was worse than execution. There was finality to execution. Those who were shot either died right away or, at least, they knew they would die and could accept it, say their prayers, be done with it all. *Twenty-Five* meant only maybe-death. Probably-death. Sometimes they were beaten to death because they couldn't make it to twenty-five, but if they survived the beating, they were probably dead anyway.

Injury in Dachau was almost always death, as surely as any minor wound meant death in the animal kingdom. An injured cat couldn't survive without human intervention, and while a wounded cat that stumbled into Dachau would perhaps be saved by an SS man, such kindness would not be shown to Jews who got *Twenty-Five*. Jews who couldn't stand at attention or slave away for hours and hours anymore.

But of course, the prisoners who got *Twenty-Five* would still try. They would suffer for days, try to cling to life even though every moment was agony. Death, when it came for them, was not a finality, it was a brutal loss of an agonizing battle.

Faust's first human had lost this battle.

Saul Waldorf didn't know why Max had given Faust's master this gruesome death sentence, and Max could not remember himself. He would have considered himself a conservative when it came to doling out deathly punishments, but he gave *Twenty-Five* too often for him to remember why he had murdered one particular man whose face he couldn't recall. Maybe Jakob had passed out from exhaustion and failed to promptly arrive in the *Appellplatz* for roll-call. Maybe he had put his frozen hands in his pockets. Maybe he had dared to look a German in the eye.

Saul didn't know why Jakob had been punished, but he reported with barely restrained bitterness what had happened after Jakob returned to their shared barrack. The teenager had tried to live after that beating, clinging to the tiny probability that he might have the strength to pull through even though the skin on his back hung off of him like ribbons and he couldn't lie down and sleep without agonizing pain. He dragged himself across Dachau, spilling his blood everywhere, trying to live.

He died, Saul said, a few days later, collapsing into the dirt during work duty.

And then he was dragged to the crematorium.

And now, his ash was spread across Dachau.

And poor little Faust, with only his nose to guide him, had been wandering about Dachau for days and days, sniffing, searching. Whiffing blood and ash, being driven to sorrow and frustration because his human was everywhere and yet he couldn't find him.

And when Max realized this, his heart stalled, his palms became sweaty, and for a few moments, he could barely breathe because his throat was tight and his brain felt like it had been turned off.

When he regained his composure enough to speak, Max dismissed Saul from his presence, whispering in a trembling tone that he would get extra bread for his cooperation. The prisoner nodded and thanked his friend's murderer, refusing to hide the disdain in his voice.

MAX'S FRIENDS AND COMRADES HAD ONCE MOCKED HIM for his preference for cats over dogs, accusing the feline species of disloyalty.

Soon, however, Faust proved them wrong. Cats could love just as thoroughly as dogs. Cats could mourn just as dogs did.

Faust was a stubborn little fellow, but eventually, he must have realized that the smell of Jakob was fading as the ground devoured his ash and rainfall washed away his blood. And when he realized that, he realized that Jakob was gone.

And when he realized that his human was dead, Faust became utterly despondent. He stopped sleeping in the sink and took to laying on the hard, cold floor. He stopped kneading Max's uniform. He stopped playing with the cat toys that Jochen brought him. He stopped stealing croissants. He stopped going outside.

When the cat stopped eating, Max began to panic. When he tried to grab Faust and take him to the vet, however, the feline ran from him. A cat that did not wish to be caught was much harder to snatch than a Jew fleeing a Nazi's grasp, and Faust was an expert at hiding. When Max managed to track him down, it was only because he heard the cat's soft, pained mewling.

"Faust, come out," he begged, peeking behind the

ELYSE HOFFMAN

couch where the cat had hidden. He reached in, trying to snag the feline by the scruff of his neck. Faust did not scratch or bite or hiss. His eyes simply glowed with a sorrowfully accusatory aura as he backed away from Max's fingers and let out that meow again, that meow which meant Jakob Beckhardt. "Mrerow..."

"Come on, Faust!" Max pleaded, rising to his feet and grabbing hold of the sofa. He started to move it, but Faust suddenly bolted out from behind the couch, flying right past Max and nearly tripping Jochen as the other SS guard came marching into the room.

"Jesus! Are you sure that cat hasn't eaten for days?" Jochen cried.

"Grab him, please!" Max begged, dropping the couch and beginning to chase the feline. Jochen shook his head, blockading the doorway with his body.

"Cat's already gone, and we don't have all day to chase him around. We were both supposed to be on duty ten minutes ago, Max," Jochen sighed, gesturing pointedly to the SS marking on his lapel, as though to remind Max of the duties that he was neglecting by chasing the depressed feline all throughout their quarters.

"But—" Max started to say, trying to look over Jochen's shoulder, worry battering his heart worse than it had when he had gotten a call from his mother informing him of Tiger's ill health.

"Look," Jochen declared, giving his friend a slight push away from the doorway. "The Kommandant's not going to be happy if you skip out on work because you're chasing a damn cat around the place."

"He's *not* a damn cat!" Max objected, returning

26

Jochen's shove with a push of his own that made his friend sigh and roll his eyes.

"You sound like a little boy," Jochen said, gesturing towards the door to the outside. "Toughen up. We have work to do."

Work, yes. Important work. Max needed to get to Dachau, to guard and beat and kill all of the Jakob Beckhardts who dared to act human for a moment. To send them to Jochen for *Twenty-Five*.

"Your fault," Max grumbled so quietly that his friend couldn't have possibly discerned his words. It *was* Jochen's fault, after all. Max had only sent Jakob to his friend's workstation, but it was always Jochen that beat the prisoners. If Faust starved himself to death, it would be Jochen's fault, of course…

"Sorry?" Jochen's query was not affronted, but laced with concern as he evidently mistook Max's accusatory mumble for an utterance of pain. Max winced.

"Nothing, I'm sorry," he muttered with a sigh. It was Jochen's fault, of course, but it was Max's fault too. He had told his friend to beat Jakob Beckhardt, and Jochen had followed his orders just as loyally as Max followed those of the Kommandant and the Kommandant followed those of Heinrich Himmler and Heinrich Himmler followed those given by Hitler himself. It was a chain of fault that had led to Jakob's death and Faust's suicidal sorrow, and if Max had only chosen to be a broken link, then Faust would not be so miserable.

"Listen," Jochen sighed, reaching out and giving his friend a pat on the shoulder. "I'm concerned about the cat, but we can wrangle him later tonight. We can't put off our job for him."

"But—"

"He's not going to starve to death in the next eight hours," Jochen noted. "He's chubby enough from eating croissants and chicken."

A decent point. Unlike all of the prisoners that Max would go count for roll-call, it was unlikely that chubby little Faust would simply fall over dead.

"All right..." Max conceded. "But you have to help me after work, help me wrangle him. Deal?"

"Deal. Promise. Swear to the Führer. Now, come on! The Kommandant will have our hides if we're late!"

The Kommandant didn't have their hides because the Kommandant himself was too busy on a phone call with Heinrich Himmler to notice two tardy SS men.

Max's workday at Dachau should have been pleasant enough: then Kommandant was occupied, the weather was good, his friends were cheerful, his favorite march was playing over the intercom system. Only a few people dropped dead during roll-call. Only a few dared to tuck their hands in their pockets or look up. Only a few needed to be punished.

At first, Max hesitated to say *Twenty-Five* to those few prisoners because he thought of Faust, but the eyes of his comrades were upon him. If he didn't say *Twenty-Five*, they would think he was weak, a Jew-sympathizer, a little boy who let the feelings of stupid animals get in the way of his duties. He said *Twenty-Five* with a hoarse voice and tried not to wince when he heard the strikes Jochen gave his victims echo about the camp.

It should have been an easy day at work, but the Nazi music blaring from the radio, Hitler's voice bellowing about the plague of Jewry, and the sounds of *smack,*

smack, smack accompanied by desperate counting made Max dizzy. At certain points, he was sure that he heard a "meow" and would turn about, hoping that Faust had forgiven him and forgotten Jakob, but he would only be greeted by another hollow-eyed man with a yellow star. Another faceless subhuman.

As he stood guard outside of the punishment barrack, gritting his teeth harder and harder as he listened to a man he had damned try to count to twenty-five, Max started thinking. The SS discouraged thinking. "I don't think, I'm an SS man," the saying went among his friends. Hitler was supposed to do their thinking for them, and they were supposed to obey with the readiness and thoughtlessness of a trained hound.

It was easy not to think when one was busy lording himself over subhumans, hitting and spitting and screaming, but Max felt no desire to approach any of Jakob Beckhardt's fellows. He stood outside of the punishment barrack, rigid as a post, and found that when he couldn't abuse a prisoner, he had little else to do except *think.*

He had never *thought* very much about the prisoners as individuals. It was impossible, really. Shaved and donning striped uniforms, differentiated only by their numbers and whichever badges they happened to bear, they all look like identical non-humans. Trying to differentiate one from another was like trying to pick one particular ant from a swarm.

As he stared out at the mass of identical subhumans, Max found himself wondering how many of them had pets at home. Maybe a few were dog people, some preferred cats, a few may have had both or maybe a bird or a lizard instead.

As Hitler bellowed on about the supposed crimes of world Jewry, his deep voice echoing about the loud-speakers, Max kept on thinking. He wondered how many of the prisoners here, whatever their crime against the state—subterfuge or a joke or merely existing as a Jew—had a pet at home that mourned them as much as Faust mourned Jakob.

He had been trained to regard the Jews as worthless animals to be killed and abused at whim, but Max loved animals, and the thought of hurting so many in his quest against the subhumans made his gut roil.

He heard another hard *smack*, another scream. A part of him, the soft part that knew how upset Faust would have been if he heard Jakob scream like that, urged him to step towards the door and ask Jochen to stop.

He didn't, though. He stood in place and didn't look when the prisoner was dragged out with his skin flayed. He stood rigid and tried to make his heart hard as iron. He tried to banish all of the weak, empathetic thoughts buzzing about his skull.

It would be all right. He would catch Faust, take him to the vet, make him better. In time, the cat would forget his Jewish master, and Max wouldn't have to think about all of this anymore.

NORMALLY, AFTER A LONG DAY OF GUARDING DACHAU, Max and his friends would march to town in a pack, laughing and joking and sharing cigarettes as they made their way to the bar. The second he was off the clock today, however, Max grabbed Jochen and forced him to bolt back to the guards' quarters.

"You promised!" Max noted when Jochen bellyached about being rushed. "We're taking Faust to the vet! You can go out for drinks after."

"I promised, right," Jochen conceded with a sigh. "All right, let's find him."

Finding Faust, however, proved to be an unfortunately easy task: the two SS men traipsed into the barrack and discovered the cat right away, lying in the middle of the carpet, twitching and squeaking with pain.

To Max, it seemed like he teleported: one moment he was standing in the doorway, staring slack-jawed at the dying cat, and the next he was bursting into the vet's office and begging her to save his poor little pet, all SS dignity forgotten as he bawled like a little boy.

"What's wrong with him?" he cried as the vet laid the cat down on the table and frantically rushed to gather her supplies.

"Has his behavior changed at all?" she queried. "Cats can hide their symptoms."

"He stopped eating three days ago, but he's not starving..."

"Liver failure, then," the vet diagnosed with a shake of her head as she pulled a syringe from a drawer. "Cats can go quickly if they stop eating. Excessive accumulation of fat occurs in the liver and..."

The vet explained why Faust was dying after that, but Max barely heard her. He could only look into the cat's glassy golden eyes and beg him not to die.

"I'm sorry, Faust, I didn't..." Max muttered, but then his SS training reared up, bringing with it a wave of frustration as he snapped, "Come on, Faust, it was just a Jew!"

Faust, in response to that, only let out a small rumble, a weak imitation of the "meow" he had reserved for Jakob. The light started to leave the cat's eyes. With horror, Max realized that the cat was dying, and the last thing he would ever hear was Max yelling, Max dismissing Jakob's life.

"Wait, I didn't..."

"Sir, please stand aside!"

"I didn't mean that, I...!"

"Please, sir, if you want me to be able to do anything, stand aside!" The vet shoved the SS man out of the way and got to work, and all Max could do was stand at a distance, trembling and praying that the cat would live.

He didn't. Ten minutes later, the vet pronounced Faust dead.

An SS man wasn't supposed to cry at the death of his own wife and children, much less the death of a cat. But Max, who felt his heart and mind shatter simultaneously as the little cat died because of him, broke down sobbing and didn't care at all what the vet thought of him for it.

"Your behavior is unacceptable."

Hardly had Max Schrader stepped through the threshold of the Kommandant of Dachau's office when he was greeted by this remark. The next twenty minutes were spent with him standing before the Kommandant's desk as his chief lambasted him.

"For the last week and a half you have been acting like a child!" the Kommandant screamed, ramming a fist on his desk. There was a bust of Adolf Hitler's head resting on the edge of the table. It trembled and swayed as though the Führer himself was shaking his head in disgust.

"You've been slacking off on your duties!"

Max nodded once. He had, of course. It had been a week and a half since Faust's death, and he still felt like he was dreaming. Or, rather, having an extended nightmare where his cat was dead and his worldview was dying.

"You have consistently overlooked prisoner misconduct—!"

He had. For the last week and a half, Max had refused to yell at the Jews or give any prisoner *Twenty-Five*. He had let prisoners tuck their hands into their pockets, cover their ears while the music blared, and look him right in the eye during roll-call. For a week and a half, Max had not treated them as subhumans.

"Unacceptable!" the Kommandant snapped. "This *alone* would be unacceptable, and yet, in addition, your fellow SS men have reported that you've been *crying* on duty!"

He had. When he thought he heard Faust's meow. When he heard Jochen giving a prisoner *Twenty-Five*. When the music and Hitler's screaming grew too loud and he realized that the sounds he had once adored were onerous now because they just reminded him of what he had done to his cat, to his cat's human. To a man that had sat with Faust and fed Faust and loved Faust just like he did.

The Kommandant kept at it, threatening and demeaning, and as he did so, Max realized with an overwhelming wave of nausea that he was stuck in the pose of the prisoners: the subhuman pose, hands at sides, legs together, head bowed. A pose that Jakob had been forced to adopt. A pose that he may have been killed for breaking.

The Kommandant was spitting, snarling like a rabid dog, screaming at Max to forget his worthless cat because they had important work to do.

And Max wanted to yell that Faust had not been a worthless cat. He wanted to scream *you're wrong, I'm wrong, all of this is wrong, we're wrong* because only now did he truly feel like he had killed a man and not a creature lower than an animal. Empathy overwhelmed indoctrination, and he wanted to scream and smash Hitler's bust, but instead he numbly declared, "Yes, Kommandant. I'm sorry, Kommandant. I'll do better, Kommandant."

The Kommandant accepted his apology. "For the Führer, straighten up!" he snapped, pointing to the statue on the desk. "Heil Hitler!"

Max said, "Heil Hitler." He hated saying it. That meant it was all over.

He left the Kommandant's office, and though he could hardly stand the grounds of Dachau anymore—the screams, the smells, the lies echoing from the loudspeakers—he forced himself to bear it long enough to journey to the place where he had murdered Jakob.

Max entered the punishment barrack and was

grateful that nobody was getting *Twenty-Five.* Jochen was there, sitting on the bench where he had beaten Jakob, humming along with the Nazi march on the radio and fiddling with his bullwhip. Max wished that he could have simply foisted everything onto Jochen, made him into the irredeemable villain, but he simply couldn't. Jochen regarded him with a look of genuine concern, and Max found that he couldn't hate him because every bit of hatred he had was now reserved for himself.

"Hey, Jochen," he said, and his friend hopped down, tossed his bullwhip onto the blood-covered table, and scurried to his friend's side.

"That asshole Heinz," Jochen said. "I figured out that *he* told the Kommandant you'd been crying. I'm gonna put something real nasty in his drink tonight."

Max smiled even though smiling in this awful place felt agonizing. "Ha...thanks, but it's fine. Just got chewed out."

"You okay? I really can't believe Heinz went and reported you for that. Your cat *just* died."

"It's fine..."

"Listen, you know...I'm really sorry about that, I mean, I didn't know cats could go that fast, I've never had one, I only have dogs..."

Max wondered what Jochen would say if he knew the entire story of why the cat had stopped eating. Would he feel so guilty then? For his friend's feelings, perhaps, but for Jakob? Max shook his head. "Don't worry. I'm not mad at you."

"Good, I..." Jochen squirmed and glanced down at his dusty jackboots. "I mean, in your place, if someone dragged me away from my dogs and they died, I'd be furious. I was sort of worried."

Jochen was a teenager like Max, like Jakob, like Saul. None of them should have been in this place.

"I don't hate you," Max said, certain that he wasn't lying. He didn't hate Jochen. He hated what this place and this country had turned him and his friends into.

"Thanks," Jochen sighed with a smile. "If you need anything..."

"Two things, actually," Max declared. "There's a Jew here named Saul Waldorf. If you could...get him out, or even just make sure he's not treated too badly. Don't give him *Twenty-Five*, maybe slip him a croissant. He's a...cat expert. Helped me with Faust a few times. I owe him."

"Oh!" Jochen's eyes glistened with surprised suspicion for a moment. He glanced about to make sure that they were not being watched and then leaned close to his friend. "Not a problem. Happens all the time, someone owes something. Hans, you know, he takes bribes from the Jews and gives 'em extra food. I'll keep tabs on your Jew. What's his number?"

Max told him, thanked him, and then heaved a heavy sigh and said, "I'm...not feeling great after that shit with the Kommandant and...everything else. I wanna go home for a spell, just for a day. Can you cover for me? I'm gonna go and catch the first train."

"Yeah, sure! I mean, your parents are in Munich, right?"

Max nodded.

"Got it! Yeah, I can cover for a day," Jochen vowed with a smile. "Say hi to your mama for me. Bring me back some of those cookies she makes."

"I will."

"You'll be back...tomorrow, or the day after?"

"Day after at latest."

"I've got your back! Feel better, Max! See you Friday!"

"See you Friday."

Max Schrader walked through the lying gates of Dachau that day and never returned.

The End

A NOTE TO MY READERS...

Thank you for reading *A Cat at Dachau*! If you enjoyed it, please tell your friends. I'd love to hear your thoughts on *A Cat at Dachau*, and reviews help authors a great deal, so I'd be very grateful if you would post a short review on Amazon and/or Goodreads. If you'd like to read more stories like this and get notifications about free and discounted books and short stories, follow me on Twitter, Facebook, Amazon, and sign up for my newsletter at elysehoffman.com! You can also follow me on Bookbub!

ALSO BY ELYSE HOFFMAN:

Where David Threw Stones: A Haunting WW2 Tale of Courage, Love, and Redemption

---

☆☆☆☆☆ "If you enjoy reading WWII historical fiction and are looking for something a little different, this is the book for you." – Michael Reit, author of "Beyond the Tracks"

West Germany, 1968

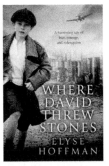

When ten-year-old David Saidel's parents are murdered, he is sent to live with his grandfather in the anti-Semitic village of Brennenbach. Miserable and lonely, David finds solace in his kindly Grandpa Ernst, who has one strict rule: never go out after midnight.

When David breaks curfew to search for his missing dog, he discovers why Ernst is so serious about his curfew: Brennenbach is cursed. When midnight strikes, the town is thrown back to 1943, the height of Hitler's reign.

The Nazi ghosts that infest Brennenbach are just as dangerous as they were in life. They're hunting for David, thinking he is the last member of a family they've been ordered to destroy.

Through the help of a little girl named Maria Rahm, David sets out to end the Curse before it claims more victims.

Award-winning author Elyse Hoffman has crafted an expertly woven tale of World War II's horrors - perfect for readers of Marcus Zusak's "The Book Thief," or Michael Reit's "Beyond the Tracks."

Fracture: A Heart-Wrenching Story of Forbidden Love and Torn Allegiances

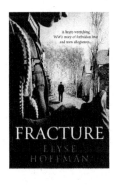 Franz Keidel is a monstrous SS soldier: loyal, hateful, and devoted to Hitler. With a cold heart, he hunts down his Führer's enemies, but one fateful mission will fracture his shield of ice.

While hunting for Jews, Franz stumbles across a familiar face: Amos Auman, his childhood friend. Amos is the only source of joy in Franz's life, but he is also a Jew. Unable to bring himself to kill his friend, Franz vows to protect Amos from his fellow Nazis.

As Franz spends more time with Amos, bringing him food and books, he falls in love with his kind-hearted friend. How could he fall in love with a man, a Jew? How can he continue to hate Jews when a Jew has thawed his icy heart?

And what will Franz do if he has to choose between Amos and his loyalty to Hitler? What choices does he have when he is already beyond redemption?

"An otherworldly tale with indelible characters in a realistic wartime setting. Hoffman's novel sublimely fuses world history and Jewish folk-lore."---Kirkus Reviews

"A truly unique work of fantastical, historical fiction set in Nazi Germany that will keep readers engaged and invested in the characters and their fates."---Booklife by Publisher's Weekly

In the fires of World War II, a child must save his people from darkness...

Ten-year-old Uriel has always been an outcast. Born mute in a Jewish village known for its choir, he escapes into old stories of his people, stories of angels and monsters. But when the fires of the Holocaust consume his village, he learns that the stories he writes in his golden notebook are terrifyingly real.

In the aftermath of the attack, Uriel is taken in by Uwe, a kind-hearted linguist forced to work for the commander of the local Nazi Police, the affably brutal Major Brandt. Uwe wants to keep Uriel safe, but Uriel can't stay hidden. The angels of his tales have come to him with a dire message: Michael, guardian angel of the Jewish people, is missing. Without their angel, the Jewish people are doomed, and Michael's angelic brethren cannot search for him in the lands corrupted by Nazi evil.

With the lives of millions at stake, Uriel must find Michael and free him from the clutches of the Angel of Death...even if that means putting Uwe in mortal danger.

The Book of Uriel is a heartbreaking blend of historical fiction and Jewish folklore that will enthrall fans of *The Book Thief* and *The World That We Knew.*

Barrack Five: A Prize Winning Holocaust Story

Winner of the 2021 Readers' Favorite Silver Medal for Short Stories.

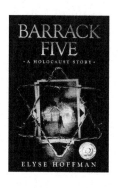

The ghosts of the past don't always stay silent...

When Vilém Rehor takes a security job at a former concentration camp, he assumes it will be dreary, but uneventful. But when someone starts carving their name onto the walls of Barrack Five, his supposedly boring job becomes more than he bargained for.

Though he tries to catch the vandal, Vilém can't figure out how they're making their marks—he never sees anyone, but that doesn't mean he's alone...

As he delves deeper into the mystery of the vandal, he realizes that the Holocaust isn't over for everyone. The spirit of a girl long gone reveals herself, desperate to be heard.

Can Vilém help this restless soul?

Printed in Great Britain
by Amazon